Lena Anderson

HEDGEHOG, PIG, and the Sweet Little Friend

Translated by Joan Sandin

R&S BOOKS
Stockholm New York London Adelaide Toronto

One night, Hedgehog was sitting and crocheting,
and all seemed cozy and right.
Her tea was lovely and hot from the pot
and her baby tucked in for the night.

She then heard the tiniest squeak from the gate.
In the darkness, she made out someone.
It was someone quite small, with sad little ears.
“I have company,” said Hedgehog. “What fun!”

So Hedgehog ran out on the step and she called,
"There's cake here, and tea! Do come in!"
But now there was nobody out by the gate.
Hedgehog hoped she would come back again.

So Hedgehog went round and searched everywhere.
She called out, "Hello there! Hello!"
But nobody answered. Where could she have gone?
thought Hedgehog. She just didn't know.

And the evening went on as evenings will go,
and Pig dropped in for a visit.
Suddenly they heard a knock on the door,
and both of them wondered, Who is it?

MORO

She stood all alone, with tears in her eyes,
and Hedgehog said, "Sweetheart, what's wrong?"
"I can't find my way home in the dark, and I'm scared.
I want Mama, and the night is so long."

“Oh, she’s so sad!” said Pig, and felt bad.
“Here’s my soup if she wants it,” he said.
And Hedgehog said kindly, “Yes, sit down, my dear,
and join us for soup and some bread.”

“First fill your tummy, then I’ll make up a bed.
We can all sleep together tonight.
Tomorrow we’ll find your mama for sure.
Don’t worry, it’ll all turn out right.

So the piglet ate up all of Pig's yummy soup.
She ate till the plate was all clean.
And then when she'd fallen asleep, Pig sighed,
"She's the cutest thing I've ever seen!"

Early next day, they all went to town.
Pig had fallen in love—it was clear.
But his new friend just sobbed, she sniffed, and she cried,
"I wish that my mama were here!"

BAKERY
PIZZA
NIZZA
Cafe

“I smell something yummy,” said Pig to his friend.
“Something sweet, like cookies and cakes!”
“Let’s run!” said the piglet. “As fast as we can!
That smell is the cakes Mama bakes!”

BAKERY
REWARD
100 SWEET ROLLS
TO THE ONE WHO
FINDS MY FIA!

There were cookies and cakes, chocolate icing and rolls,
as far as the eye could see.
The piglet ran in, crying, “Mama, look here!
I’m home! Aren’t you happy? It’s me!”

“My sweet little Fia, oh, where have you been?
I’ve searched for you all over town!

"And now that you're here, I'm so happy, my dear.
But I'll faint if I don't soon sit down."

And Pig got a hundred sweet-smelling rolls,
and his friends all pigged out on the rest.
"It's true I love sweet rolls," Pig told them all,
"but Fia's the sweet I love best!"

"My adorable Fia, my sweet sugar cone,
my sweetheart, my pink-nosed friend,
by the curl in my tail, I swear I love you!"
And now we have come to the end.

Rabén & Sjögren Bokförlag, Stockholm
www.raben.se

Originally published in Sweden by Eriksson & Lindgren under the title *Kotten, Grisen och Lilla Vännen*

Distributed in Canada by Douglas & McIntyre Ltd.
Library of Congress Control Number: 2006937900
Printed by Narayana Press, Denmark
First American edition, 2007

ISBN-13: 978-91-29-66742-4
ISBN-10: 91-29-66742-9

Rabén & Sjögren Bokförlag is part of
P. A. Norstedt & Söner Publishing Group, established in 1823